Tiny TINA

Laurence Anholt

Illustrated by Tony Ross

ORCHARD

www.anholt.co.uk

Hee, hee, hello everyone!
My name is **Ruby** and I have the
funniest family in the world.
In these books, I will introduce you
to my **freaky family**.

You will meet people like…

Bendy Ben

Brainy Boris

Mucky Micky

Poetic Polly

Hairy Harold

Brave Bruno

But this book is all about…my teeny-tiny sister, **TINA**.
We are going to meet my sister Tina, the tiniest girl in the world. But where is she?

We cannot find my sister anywhere. Perhaps Tina has gone outside to play.

Wait. Wait there. Let's get a magnifying glass.

Now we can see her. Now we can see Tina, the teeniest, weeniest, cutest girl who ever lived.

My sister Tina is so tiny that she
sleeps in a pencil case.

And has a bath in a teacup.

And goes for a ride on a
rollerskate.

Wherever she goes, people stop and smile.

My tiny sister Tina is so tiny and
so cute that everyone wants to give
her a big cuddle.

Lots of people have small brothers and sisters at home, but NO ONE is quite as small and quite as sweet as my sister Tina. That is why everybody loves her.

Tina's favourite shop is the pet
shop. The pet-shop man is tall.

Tina loves to sit on the counter or
play on a hamster wheel.

Lots of people come to the pet
shop.
They cuddle the kittens.

They hold the hamsters.

They pat the puppies.

Most of all they come to kiss Tina,
the tiniest girl in the world.

But sometimes my sister Tina gets
fed up with being small.
Especially when she gets knocked
over by a big bouncy rabbit or
when she falls into a goldfish bowl.

Then Tina says,

The man in the pet shop knows everything about looking after pets. If anyone has a problem with their pet, they ask the pet-shop man.

The pet-shop man has Tortoise Tablets for tortoises who won't wake up.

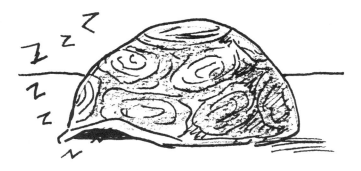

And Parrot Pills for parrots who won't talk.

One day, a lady comes in to the
shop. She has a small dog that will
not grow.
The pet-shop man looks at the little
dog. Then he gets out a bottle of
Doggy Grow Drops.

"You must be careful," says the pet-shop man. "These Doggy Grow Drops are VERY strong! If you give your dog ONE drop too many, he will grow as big as a DONKEY! If you give your dog TWO drops too many, he will grow as big as a DINOSAUR!"

The lady goes home to try the Doggy Grow Drops. My sister Tina has been listening. She has heard all about the VERY STRONG Doggy Grow Drops.

The pet-shop man is busy with a
hamster who has a headache. My
tiny sister Tina climbs onto a high
shelf and takes the bottle of Doggy
Grow Drops.

Tina opens the bottle. She needs something to try the Doggy Grow Drops on. She sees a baby woodlouse on the floor. Tina gives ONE tiny drop to the baby woodlouse.

The woodlouse begins to grow...

Up...

and up...

and UP.

Until it grows as big as a
guinea pig.

"Mmm, these Doggy Grow Drops
are quite strong," says my tiny
sister Tina.
She gives TWO of the Doggy
Grow Drops to a hamster.
The hamster begins to grow...

Up...

and up...

and UP.

Until it grows as big as a pony.

"These Doggy Grow Drops are VERY strong," says Tina, and she finishes the WHOLE BOTTLE! My tiny sister Tina begins to grow…

Up…

and up…

and UP!

We are going to meet my sister
Tina again.
But where is she?

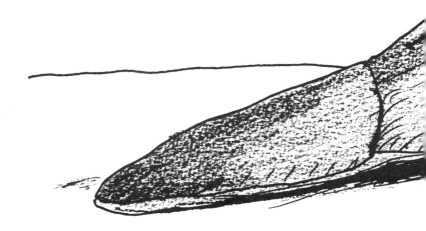

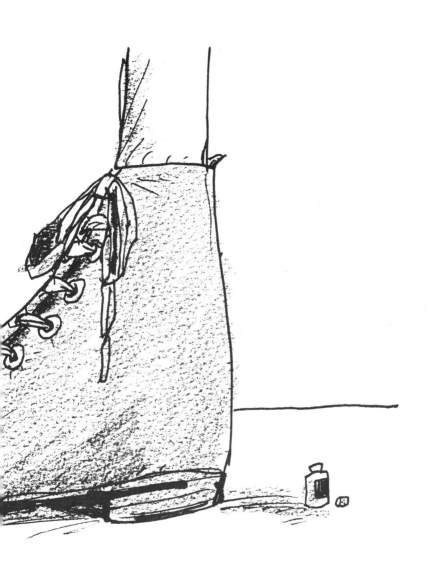

We cannot see Tina anywhere. Perhaps she has gone outside to play.

39

Quick! Run and get a helicopter.

Now we can see her. Now we can
see my sister Tina, the BIGGEST,
most ENORMOUS girl who ever
lived.

Tina is bigger than a cow. Tina is bigger than a camel. Tina is bigger than KING KONG!

Where are you going? Why is everybody running away? Don't you want to kiss Tina any more?

The man from the pet shop comes
running. He has a big box. It is a
box of VERY strong Pink Shrink
Poodle Powder.

He gives Tina one spoonful.

Tina begins to shrink…

Down…

and down…

and down.

Now here is Tina next to the
counter in the pet shop.

My sister Tina is not too big.
My sister Tina is not too small.
My sister Tina is exactly the
right size.
And everybody loves her.

THE END

My FREAKY FAMILY

COLLECT THEM ALL!

RUDE RUBY	978 1 40833 639 7
MUCKY MICKY	978 1 40833 764 6
POETIC POLLY	978 1 40833 754 7
BRAINY BORIS	978 1 40833 756 1
BRAVE BRUNO	978 1 40833 762 2
TINY TINA	978 1 40833 760 8
BENDY BEN	978 1 40833 758 5
HAIRY HAROLD	978 1 40833 752 3

Also available as an ebook